FICTIONAL PLANNING

www.mascotbooks.com

Fictional Planning: A Novella

Cover illustration by Seth Miller

For more information, please contact:
Mascot Books, an imprint of Amplify Publishing Group
620 Herndon Parkway, Suite 220
Herndon, VA 20170
info@mascotbooks.com

Library of Congress Control Number: 2023923516
CPSIA Code: PRV0424A
ISBN-13: 979-8-89138-093-6

Printed in the United States

To all the dedicated teachers who took the time to share their thoughts about, views on, and histories in education.

JOHN CONTRATTI

FICTIONAL PLANNING

A NOVELLA

MASCOT BOOKS

WTF

Courtney Reynolds gingerly sipped on her glass of white wine. A big sigh accompanied her first swallow as a sense of calm and peacefulness washed over her. She loved these special moments in her life. She had turned thirty-three two days ago. It was a quiet birthday, just the way she liked it. And for the moment, she hadn't a care in the world.

Courtney loved spending warm summer nights with a handful of coworkers and friends at a local restaurant. There were so many spots to choose from, but they always gravitated toward their old stomping ground. Max's Pub was the perfect setting to sit for hours and just relax with friends over drinks and food, catching up with the latest goings-on of their friends, family, and mutual acquaintances. The conversation always followed a familiar pattern. "Did you see such-and-such movie?" "I just started watching this new show on Netflix." "Did you see that picture so-and-so posted on Facebook?" "What plans do you have for your next vacation?" And after the usual questions and their answers, the conversation always returned to work. It couldn't be avoided. It was the strongest bond they shared.

As the conversation continued, the server came to take their orders. Courtney stared at his unusually tall physique. She always allowed her friends to order first. She relished, just for the moment, hearing what each of them chose. And then, as always, Courtney would order the market salad with no red onions and the cedar-plank salmon. She always thought it was best to stick with what you know. "If it ain't broke, don't fix it," was her motto.

On the very rare occasions when she decided to be daring and order something new, it never seemed to work out well for her. So, she determined, a salad and salmon was the way to go.

As their conversation continued, a thunderous crash sounded in the distance. The abrupt sound made Courtney jump. Her body twisted and turned. As fast as she heard the noise, she quickly noticed her friends hadn't jumped or even reacted to the sound. Their conversation just continued on as though nothing had happened. Courtney found that very strange. Was she hearing things?

Then all of a sudden, she couldn't hear her friends' voices. It was as if someone had a volume knob and was slowly turning it down. Their mouths were all moving, but no words were coming out. Courtney began to feel a little panicked. Then a bright flash took over the entire restaurant. Courtney was startled and quickly squinted her eyes. As quickly as the bright white appeared, it was gone. And everything around Courtney Reynolds became pitch black.

Courtney loved walking through the local bookstores. She enjoyed getting in her car, driving over, and listening to her favorite songs of the past on her journey. Give her music from the sixties and seventies, and she was in heaven. Some may call Courtney an old soul. She loved television shows from decades ago, classic films, and retro music. Bookstores were her happy place. She relished looking through the latest autobiographies of actors and actresses of today and in the past. She showed great interest in the lives of interesting celebrities, especially if they were more talented than most.

After walking up and down the aisles and reading titles and paragraphs here and there, she would make her way up the escalator to the children's section. She loved visiting the children's department in the evening. It was less crowded and much quieter. She could usually count on seeing at least one parent sitting with their child and reading to them. Courtney loved seeing this and longed to have this experience for herself one day. Her fascination with picture books sometimes became a drain on her bank account, but it was worth it. They made her happy. She was always drawn to the cleverest titles and the most exuberant illustrations.

But to Courtney, the best part of strolling through the bookstore was the cup of coffee she would order and sip throughout her visit. In her mind, it was pure bliss.

The big question was always: what should she order this time? It was always cold, but should she go basic? An iced coffee with half-and-half? Or should she splurge on a delightfully blended Frappuccino? Or was this more of an infused tea day? After giving it careful consideration, Courtney approached the overly tall barista.

She wondered why he was so tall and why she was feeling even smaller than her five-foot-six-inch frame. As she was about to give her order to "Lurch," the name she had randomly assigned him in her head, a small child showed up out of nowhere and stood right behind her. She looked around and could see there was no parent to be found. Courtney was always amazed at how some parents just allowed their children—little children—to wander away from them and roam freely through the store. If she had a child, which she hoped for one day, they would be right by her side at all times in public places. "Parents with such empty heads," she would say.

All of a sudden, this abandoned child began to scream at the top of his lungs. It made Courtney jump, and her body twisted and turned. She noticed all the people surrounding her didn't react to the screaming child. They continued to give their drink orders as if they didn't hear a thing or, for that matter, even notice there was a child standing next to them. She noticed that even Lurch had no reaction to the chaos that had just begun. Wouldn't a screaming child garner the attention of other store patrons? Was she just more sensitive to noise?

The volume of the child's bellowing got lower and lower, as if he had a knob on his back and someone was slowly reducing the volume. Then suddenly the store was illuminated with a very bright light. Courtney shut her eyes and then began to squint to test whether she could see anything. But as quickly as it had become super bright, that's how fast everything went pitch black.

Courtney Reynolds loved lying in the sun on the beach as often as she could. She would cover herself with suntan lotion from head to toe, and still she would keep herself covered with towels and light clothing. As much as she yearned for a nice tan like her friends, she always worried about her skin getting too much sun. But being at the beach was a time for her to be with her own thoughts and enjoy a moment of peaceful bliss.

While reading one of her favorite new autobiographies, which she would have purchased at the bookstore, she would occasionally pick up her phone to play a word game on one of her favorite apps. She tried not to look at her text messages while relaxing. No doubt, it would be from a friend complaining about the same thing that she had heard a hundred times already. So it was best to completely ignore any message notifications.

She would occasionally look up at the children who ran back and forth in front of her. Once in a while, she would put her book down to sip the ice-cold beverage she had purchased on her way to the beach. She would pause to think about her life. This seemed to be something she was doing more often of late. Being thirty-three and still single didn't sit well with her. It didn't sit well with her mother either. There was no lack of trying to find a husband. She dated occasionally, but Mr. Right never seemed to be on the horizon. Not yet anyway.

At the beach, she was always on high alert looking around. She had no desire to see anyone she knew, especially if they had any association with her job. With her hair up and no make-up on, she was also well aware she didn't have a "beach body." She always joked with her best friend, Carrie, that "all I have is a body that goes to the beach."

She occasionally liked to people-watch, and she would generously give them very exciting lives. In her head, they all received unique names and exotic jobs and adventures.

She usually went to the beach on the same day of the week, so she was used to seeing the same lifeguard at his post every time. But today was different. There by the lifeguard chair stood an extremely tall and thin gentleman. Courtney wondered where all these incredibly tall men were coming from. Was she shrinking?

She shook her head to clear her eyes, but just as she was about to get back to her book, a huge gust of wind blew across the beach. Sand flew into her face and, even more tragically, onto the straw of her beverage. She kept her eyes shut tightly for the duration of the brief windstorm. With them closed, a quiet calm came over her. She clearly heard the ocean waves continue to crash, one after another, onto the shore. She listened to the sound of children screaming and their parents yelling at them not to get sand in their eyes. The wind died down, and the sand stopped stinging her face, so she gingerly opened her eyes. But it was much too bright, and she quickly squeezed her eyes shut again. Then suddenly, the light that had been permeating her eyelids was gone. Her eyes flew open to see nothing. It was pitch black.

The next sound Courtney heard was very familiar, but it was unusual for the setting she was in. This was not one of the familiar beach sounds. Her eyes were sealed shut again with no light able to seep in, and she heard a persistent, loud beeping sound. *What is that noise?* she wondered. *What was going on?* The beeps seemed to grow louder and louder, and once again, her body began to jump, twist, and turn. Suddenly, she began to see little glimmers of red light sneaking through her eyelids.

Courtney Reynolds jumped up in her bed, gasping for breath. She felt slightly dizzy, and her vision was blurred. She wondered what was going on. What had just happened? Why wouldn't that beeping go away? Slowly, her eyes focused on a blinking red light on the side of her bed.

Wait a minute, it's my alarm, she thought to herself. Trying to focus her brain, she stretched her arm to hit the off button. She squinted her eyes to see the time. It was 4:46 a.m. Slowly her mind began to clear as the sleep-induced fogginess melted away. She looked all around her bedroom. She could see light from the lamppost glimmering through her bedroom curtain.

And then it hit her. Like a ton of bricks.

A resounding "Fuuuuccccckkkkkk" came flying out of her mouth. For you see, Courtney Reynolds had suddenly realized it was the first day of a new school year.

HERE WE GO AGAIN

For those not in the education field, let's just say it, "They just don't get it!" Courtney was sick and tired of her friends and relatives saying, "I'm so jealous—you have the whole summer off," and "You're so lucky you get so many days off during the year." Despite those statements being technically true, Courtney would always be ready to respond to them with the hundreds of things these "geniuses" just didn't know about teaching. In a nutshell, teachers are balancing about twenty-five little lives for ten months. That's right, *ten* months. School doesn't stop even though teachers are home on Columbus Day or for Winter Recess. The dedicated teachers are always preparing for the next day, the following week, and even when the glimmering light of summer is at their fingertips, a dedicated teacher is already planning for the next school year.

Another thing that some non-educators don't know is that the "first day" of school is not with their students. It's a "Superintendent's

Conference Day" or something similar. As Courtney would always say, "Just give me the kids, and let's skip this part of it." Like many of her fellow teachers, she had her reasons for this perspective.

Courtney always met with her friends and colleagues in the parking lot on Superintendent's Conference Day. Sharon was a twenty-four-year veteran of teaching, and Mia was now starting her second year. Sharon taught fourth grade, Courtney third, and Mia second. All three wore the same expression on their faces. It's the expression that silently mused, *Where did summer go*? Or, on some faces, it came across more like, *I can't believe we're back here again*. The weather echoed their feelings at a humid ninety degrees. The three of them took a deep breath and headed into the school's multi-purpose room.

On this day, you wouldn't see just the faculty from your own school building, you would see every employee from the district. This part of the conference was an absolute treat for the trio. Sharon, being the veteran, knew most of the people, although more new faces were starting to creep in. One starts to feel old when you can no longer name three-quarters of the room.

As they entered the multi-purpose room, the scent of coffee wafted into their nostrils. They saw groups of people standing around chatting with cups of coffee in their hands. At the other end of the room, a group hovered over the table adorned with mini bagels. Sharon was always amused by the people breathing over the bagels. To her, they were reminiscent of vicious lions, hovering over a poor, sweet zebra. Hadn't any of them seen a bagel before?

After taking in the scene, the trio felt prepared for the usual first day chitchat with their district colleagues. They subconsciously drew closer to each other, bracing for the inevitable barrage of people and meaningless conversation.

Carly was another veteran teacher who, each year, would approach Courtney immediately. A fake kiss was quickly followed by the standard "How was your summer?"

Courtney despised that question. But before she could utter one word about her very quiet and subdued summer, Carly was out of the gate spewing on about her summer vacation. As usual, Carly did lots of traveling to some of the most exotic places in the world. She then rambled out a list of all the newest and hippest restaurants she'd gone to. Carly had a wealthy husband. She didn't have to work. The whole district knew that. She was basically there to let everyone know about her outside life and show off her high-end clothes and latest accessories. As usual, when Courtney was about to reveal her "exciting" summer of reading, gardening, and doing her own cooking, Carly was already on to the next person.

Everyone knows a "Carly." She's the educator who, on the first day of school, tries to get to as many people as possible so she can tell them all about her summer. She has no interest in what anyone else has done or has to say. A year ago, when the trio returned, Sharon's dad had passed over the summer. When Carly approached Sharon on the first day of school to see how she was doing, Sharon had barely uttered four words about her grief before Carly was talking about her trip to Australia.

The sad part was that Carly was so oblivious. She had no idea how she came across to others. But everyone around saw her for who she was. She never made eye contact, because, like a panther, she was always scouting out who to pounce on next, who else to reveal details about her "amazing" life to. Superficially, everyone liked Carly, even if it was just because she was amusing and fun to gossip about. But deep down, many felt sorry for her. Many of her closest friends believed she felt empty inside. Despite the luxury of having money and being able to travel the world, she was trying to fill a void within her. Her husband traveled quite a bit, and many colleagues thought there were probably some shenanigans going on. The joke was that even if Carly thought so too, she would forget about it as soon as she caught another glimpse of her bank account.

Another common thing on the first day back was one person's new look or haircut. Usually, it was an older woman colleague who decided to "go short," as they would say. She wanted to do something "fun" with her hair. Women would gather around their female friend and gush and fuss about her new hairdo. Isn't getting a haircut a common thing? Yet, somehow, it creates a big buzz. Soon Sharon would say, "Watch, as soon as some of those women disperse, they'll be talking about their friend's new k.d. lang hairdo."

"Who?" Mia would ask. And suddenly, Sharon felt much older and disgusted.

After numerous hellos, hugs, and kisses, it was time to start Superintendent's Conference Day. On the way to find a seat, Courtney could hear the teachers wondering and complaining about whom they would have to sit and listen for ninety minutes. Courtney felt the same way most years. *Which "guru" will be presenting this morning? How many times will we have to shake our heads up and down to show that we're paying attention?* Yes, every once in a while, the staff would get lucky with an educator who was smart, interesting, and applicable, and the ninety minutes would fly by. But let's face it, Courtney and the other two hundred people there knew the odds were usually not in their favor on this annual day of torture.

Like clockwork, Sharon would lean over and say, "Do you know how much work I could be getting done right now for my students?" A good 90 percent of the audience were all thinking the same thing. As for the other 10 percent, they were settling in for a ninety-minute nap. You always knew how attention grabbing the guest speaker was by scanning the room. If most people had their phones out, most likely texting the person two seats away to say how awful the speaker was, you knew that, once again, this was another first day "tanker." It always amazed Sharon that each year a handful of staff members became groupies, for a brief moment, of the day's guest speaker. They'd follow them and tweet them and gush over how amazing they were. But once the reality of the school days hit and overwhelmed the teachers, these guest speakers become a mere memory of the past. Maybe we need to start calling these "experts" back to deal with administration, difficult colleagues, parents, and unruly students on a daily basis.

Whenever the guest speaker for the year was being introduced, the group around Sharon was ready for her, "All right, whose ass are we kissing this year?" She had long ago learned not to be impressed by the talking heads.

Once the keynote presentation is out of the way, the rest of the day is spent at grade level and faculty meetings. And most of them were simply regurgitations of the same thing year after year. They could easily be cut down to give teachers more time to set up a classroom that would wow and excite their students on the first day of school. Courtney never understood how some teachers created the most spectacular classroom environments for their students while others did nothing to excite and motivate their pupils—especially after sitting for ninety minutes hearing about motivation. The kids spend a huge chunk of each day in their classroom. It should be a place they want to be. A dedicated teacher needs to be aware of the visuals their students are surrounded by and the feelings the room evokes. No matter what the age, students need an environment that will excite them. It bothered Courtney when she would hear a colleague say that primary teachers need more time to set up their classroom than those teaching in intermediate classrooms. This was definitely not true. It really was all about the dedication of the teacher. When Courtney first came to the district, she was a permanent sub. She saw how many different teachers decorated their rooms, and it would upset her when she worked in a room that had no decorations, books, posters, etc. She longed for her own classroom to make interesting and inviting one day.

Most teachers spend an arm and a leg of their own money to create a warm learning environment for their students. Mia realized this her first year of teaching. What was in her classroom when she arrived? There was the basic furniture, consisting of desks and chairs for the students and a desk, chair, and file cabinet for the teacher. And there would be textbooks and workbooks for the students. In some cases, if you were lucky, a classroom already had a little library of paperback books for the students. Otherwise, aside from a few computers along one wall of the room, that would be it.

This is where the teacher has to make a decision. Do they want their classroom to look like a storage room or a classroom? This is where educators' out-of-pocket costs begin. Posters, picture books, extra supplies for students who don't have them, theme and holiday decorations, charts of all kinds, and dozens of other items all add up at the teacher's expense. Sure, as the year goes on, teachers create charts of their own with their students that are displayed around the classroom, but when those students enter their new classroom for the first time, they need to be wowed. Courtney must have spent thousands of dollars over the years on all the things she bought for her classroom and students. Yes, teachers do get an allowance to buy things for their classroom, but it's nowhere close to enough.

After a day of meetings, the teachers may have a little time in their classroom during regular school-day hours, if they're lucky. But most years, you can find them working on their classrooms long into the evening the day before the students arrive.

The day before the kids start school, Courtney never gets a good night's sleep. She's always too excited about the first day of school. Seeing a new bunch of fresh faces is one of her favorite things. And once again, it was time for a brand-new classroom family that would get to spend the next ten months together.

READY, SET, GO

The first day with students always felt the same to Courtney. She would enter the building way too early and be hit in the face with a blast of heat. She would always think of her students. Most of them would be coming back from weeks of swimming, playing outside, and being in their air-conditioned homes. But now these lucky little ones get to spend seven hours a day in a classroom that was inside a hot, humid school building.

If you were lucky, you could find a little space where the air conditioning worked well enough to counteract the still-hot temperatures outside. Most of the staff would hang out in one of those rare rooms for a few minutes before the day began. It was mostly to cool down after spending the past hour running around getting ready to open up their classroom for a new group of students.

"Make your teachers feel comfortable, and they'll have a good year," is what Sharon was constantly telling administration. Staff joked that was what would be engraved on her plaque when she eventually retired.

Sharon had an opinion on most things, and she was never afraid to share it. She had been doing this for a long time and had seen all types of changes to the school and the system. She would start off running on the first day of school and keep going full speed until the very last day. She was dismayed at how kids these days didn't get dressed up on the first day of school. Then again, she had quite a bit to say about her colleagues' attire, as well. "Are they coming to teach children, or are they going to happy hour?" Or, "Did she forget to run a comb through her hair this morning?" And one of her favorite lines, "Did she think today was pajama day?"

No matter what she said, 90 percent of the staff loved Sharon. She told it like it was. Yes, there were the 10 percent who didn't enjoy her. But then again, those were the people who dressed like they were going to happy hour and never put a comb through their hair.

Sharon had lots to say about administration, as well. She got along with most of them, but there was always one who was an irritant to her and vice versa. She had more respect for administrators who had put in the time. The newer, younger ones, not so much. Courtney would always tell Sharon to give new administration a break. People need time to get their feet wet and find their way in an already established school. Sharon believed, like many others, a new administrator needed to come in quietly. They should observe and be neutral with all staff members. Don't come in and announce, "change is good," because you won't last very long. Sharon was a big believer in growing and learning. She took courses after school and was always watching educational webinars online. Even so, "If it ain't broke, don't fix it," was a motto she shared with Courtney.

Sharon was always leery of the new administration relying on certain staff members to help them with things or lead a committee. Sometimes the choice would be a good one, but often enough it would be a poor decision—one that would baffle the entire building. Was the administrator being savvy by keeping a possible enemy close, or were they just an idiot? Usually, it was the latter. A staff member who had an agenda would cozy up to a new administrator. And the other teachers could tell when one got a little too cozy. When an administrator is letting specific colleagues take charge of certain tasks within the building, ones they never did before, it was usually a clear sign that shenanigans between the two were going on.

Courtney and Mia would turn bright red over their lunches when Sharon would tell them about certain staff members having relationships with administrators over the years. Sometimes, Mia would exclaim that her lunch was now ruined after hearing that bit of news. She didn't need those kinds of pictures in her head. Sharon had seen quite a bit and knew of even more during her twenty-four years in the district. "People come and go, but I'm still here," she would always say.

Meeting her new class always excited Courtney. It was extra special when she had a lot of siblings from previous students. It felt familiar and comfortable. She loved seeing many of the parents whose children she had taught in the past, and she also enjoyed when she got to see her students from the previous year.

The first day of school always flies by. First, it takes time for the students to unpack and get settled. Most students like to share what they did over the summer, and most teachers like to talk about the new school year as well. If you're lucky, maybe a few activities will be completed as well. But before you know it, the bell rings, and the first day of school has come and gone.

By dismissal, both students and staff are ready to call it a day. You can see exhaustion and beads of sweat on their faces when they push open the door to dismiss the class. A day that's filled with activity is always the key element for kids to be motivated and learn. You could always count on one of the teachers saying, "One hundred seventy-nine days to go," as everyone exited the building. There would be another one hundred seventy-nine days in the lives of teachers all across the country.

PARTNERS

The education field attracts a variety of personalities. You either adapt to it, go with it, or ignore it. Fifth-grade teachers Anna and Alice did all three.

Everyone liked Anna and Alice. They were grade-level partners who were great colleagues and close friends. And they were work-horses. Even though they had been teaching the same grade for years, they made sure that every year, fifth grade was a blast for the students. They were two women in their fifties with similar lives. They had professional husbands, kids in college, kids getting married, and lately, a few grandchildren. They were friendly and always happy to help when needed, but they generally kept to themselves. It was always best to let people come and look for you in school. It wasn't a good idea to be the teacher who was always pestering administration with nonsense.

Anna and Alice taught in the two classrooms at the end of the hallway on the second floor. They called their floor heaven, as they knew the floor below them could be quite hellish. Courtney, Sharon, and Mia were also happy to be on the heaven level, even though they were at the opposite end of the hall.

Anna and Alice were both cultured, comparatively speaking. No way would they be able to talk about the latest shows they'd watched on Masterpiece with some of the younger staff members. Let's just say they were more Turner Classic Movies and PBS, while many of the teachers in "hell" were more, shall we say, Bravo.

They could have been a little snooty with their "cultured life," but instead they remembered everyone's birthday and wedding anniversary, and they would always follow up to ask about a colleague's ailing child or parent. Courtney called them "two class acts," and that's exactly what they were. Anna and Alice were filled with great wisdom, and staff appreciated their advice and suggestions. But the administration tended to do the opposite. Both Alice and Anna were starting to feel that the administration was more interested in the suggestions from the newer and younger staff. It was quite obvious at times and often disappointing for many of the experienced teachers, but Anna and Alice didn't worry about it.

Even though they were in heaven, they somehow always knew what was going on in all areas of the building. With them it never seemed like gossip. Somehow, even when Sharon told the same story as one of them had, it always seemed more salacious, even though it was all true. Courtney believed it was all in the tone and delivery.

Some of the people from hell would wander up to heaven once in a while. If you had a problem, whether it was a situation at home or at work, Anna and Alice were the go-to healers. Their advice was always sound, and it was up to the individual to take it or not. The smart ones usually did. But one day they were very cautious about handling what had risen up through the floorboards from below.

Corinne was a sweet, quiet teacher who, for years, had wanted to get out of hell and go to heaven. But each year, administrators would tell her the same story, “You’re such a wonderful primary teacher.” That was it. Once they said that, you knew you weren’t getting what you wanted. Administrators always know best, don’t they? Once you’re labeled, it sticks.

It was about thirty minutes before students were to arrive at school, and Anna and Alice were having their morning coffee. They were early birds. They never understood how some teachers just walked in swinging their pocketbooks at the exact time when school was about to start. Anna and Alice would walk up the stairs like “two jackasses,” as they would refer to themselves, hauling the bags of work they’d lugged home the night before. And never get them started on teachers who never got to school on time, and nothing was ever done about it.

With their large Starbucks coffees, they would sit together going over plans for the day and chatting about something they’d both watched the night before on television. On this particular morning, Corrine’s face peeked through the glass panel as she knocked on Anna’s door. The pair were always welcoming and offered warm smiles as they waved her in. Corinne entered with a cheery hello. She asked how they were, and they asked how her four kids were doing. It seemed like every time you turned around, Corinne had a new baby on the way. But she vowed that she has closed up shop. “No more babies!” she exclaimed. Nobody believed her. Everyone foresaw another trip to buybuy BABY in their future. You didn't need a crystal ball to predict that.

Anna and Alice could see that something was on Corinne's mind, and she needed to get it off her chest before she exploded. "What's going on?" Anna asked. At that moment, Courtney popped open the door. She was quite used to seeing that certain look on people's faces when you walk into a room, and all goes silent. She quickly retreated, saying she would come back later.

As the door closed, Corinne blurted out that she couldn't stand any of her colleagues down in hell anymore.

Anna and Alice knew exactly what she was talking about. They had seen it for years, and some of the newer people fit right in. It always amazed them how easily new teachers could fall into the trap of believing everything they hear about fellow colleagues. You could always count on one viper to badmouth a coworker for no reason other than their own insecurities and jealousies. A smart newcomer would take everything they hear with a grain of salt and make their own observations and conclusions as time goes by. The problem was that while individually—for the most part—the people in hell were nice, as a whole they were just awful. Plain and simple, they were not nice people. What was even more scary was that they all believed they had each other's back. Anna and Alice knew all too well that this wasn't the case.

Once a month, Anna and Alice would have dinner with one of their hellion friends, which no one knew about. The two ladies would just sit back, glasses of wine in their hands, and listen to their fellow colleague rip apart the same people she'd had lunch with approximately six hours earlier. Anna and Alice were sadly accustomed to this. The behavior of some of their colleagues were atrocious. When they had to venture into hell, they never knew who would grant them a hello or good morning. They would fare much better if they ran into one teacher at a time, but if the hellions were in a pack, a fellow teacher could be hemorrhaging on the floor, and they wouldn't give her the time of day.

"Tell us about it, Corrine," Alice invited.

Corinne explained that she was so tired of her colleagues downstairs always talking behind her back.

Anna gently asked, "Are you sure?"

Alice figured Anna was just being polite. They both knew it was true. The ladies who lunched together would spend much of their mealtime ripping Corinne apart. Corinne never ate in the teachers' room. She spent her lunch period working or running to the grocery store to buy food for her family. That's right, her family. She had a family, just like they did. And her not being in the teachers' room gave the "Witches of Eastwick"—one of Sharon's names for them—ample opportunity to spew their venom and rip her apart. Their favorite catchphrases included, "She's a terrible teacher," "She has no control of the class," and "She doesn't know what she's doing."

Corinne said she was absolutely sure, and Alice and Anna knew she was right. They had heard it numerous times. The biggest—and saddest—joke was that it was coming from people who should have been the *last* ones to be judging any of the other teachers.

Corinne explained that she always felt it, and when she would walk in on them devouring their lunches, she could feel the whole tone of the room change. One of the piranhas would always say, "Oh hi, Corinne." Did they really think they were fooling anyone?

So how could Corinne be 100 percent sure? Alice and Anna were hoping to put a little doubt in Corinne's mind so she wouldn't feel quite as bad. But there was no denying this one.

"Do you know Ariana, the student teacher downstairs?" Corinne asked. Anna and Alice both knew Ariana. She had worked with Courtney in third grade a few weeks before, and they all had lunch on various occasions.

"Yes," said Alice. "She's a lovely girl."

"Well," said Corinne, "she's my mom's best friend's daughter." Anna and Alice looked at each other then quickly away. They immediately realized things were going to be heating up in hell quite soon, because they knew exactly what Corinne was about to say.

THE BULLIES AREN'T ON THE PLAYGROUND

In most schools, after recess has ended, students are returning to class, you can always see a colleague standing outside their classroom door talking to a group of students. It's usually a group of girls, but not always. Sometimes the boys like to get in the mix.

Courtney was used to this. The offense was usually very minor. Something like "She said she doesn't want to be my friend," "She's talking about me to other kids," "She keeps following me at recess," or "She said I couldn't play in the group." Now there are some teachers who give this daily nonsense *way* too much time and attention. And others, like Courtney, "nip it in the bud," as she learned from Barney Fife. (And if you don't know who Barney Fife is, Sharon wouldn't be happy with you.)

Courtney knew her students had big feelings and was always aware of it. If ever there was a serious offense, she would take it seriously and handle it carefully.

If you were Sharon, you would offer a quick retort to the nonsense and get back to teaching. Everyone's favorite Sharonism was, "So she doesn't want to be your friend? Good, you'll save on birthday gifts." Most of the time, the kids wouldn't have a clue what she was saying, but there's always that one student teachers adore, because they get their sarcasm and sense of humor. Those are the students you always remember.

But for the most part, the students were generally good little boys and girls. Unfortunately, the more poorly behaved sometimes became the adults and the colleagues you work with each day.

Anna and Alice knew this latest news from Corinne was going to upset the apple cart down in hell. For a person who was supposedly a bad teacher, had no control, and was sometimes called weird, she certainly knew what she was doing when it came to putting an end to the bullying from her peers.

It turns out Corinne deliberately didn't want anyone to know that she knew the student teacher, Ariana. Corinne, Ariana, and their families had spent New Year's Day together every year since Ariana was a little girl. It would be best to not let it get around. That's always a big mistake in school districts. It's usually best not to say who you know when you get a job in the district. You could be the most talented individual, but behind your back the rest of the staff will only refer to you knowingly with a title relating to the person you know in the district. She's Jan's cousin, Bill's niece, Mary's podiatrist's daughter, or Bill's landscaper's son. You get the picture.

"How do you know what they said about you?" asked Anna. Corinne told Anna and Alice that Ariana eats lunch with the members from hell every day. Since Corinne never ate in the faculty room, it made her the topic of conversation on most days. Ariana would just sit there and take it all in. She never revealed to her cooperating teacher that she had a connection to Corinne. If Corinne wasn't the topic of the day, they would happily tear apart other colleagues and, of course, administration, as well. The Witches of Eastwick were equal opportunists.

Antionette Marshal was the most notorious of the bunch. She had been teaching second grade for twenty-four years, just like Sharon. They had started the same year, and initially they became close friends. But when Sharon got a whiff of Antionette skewering her one day, that friendship came to an abrupt end. Administrators were well aware that they could never put them on the same grade level, and they were best kept on different floors in the building.

That's what many teachers don't understand. You just never know who talks with whom. It's quite common to be teaching on a grade level with someone who is constantly badmouthing a colleague from a different grade level. Then a few years later, those two people are working together on a grade level, and they become besties. How eye-opening, if someone were to approach their unsuspecting grade-level partner and fill them in on what their new best friend used to say about them all those previous years. Needless to say, it would be quite a shock.

For too many in education, there's no loyalty, only survival.

Antionette was a very proud Christian woman. She made sure that everyone saw the cross that hung around her neck each day. But

Sharon was right on the money when it came to Antionette. She was simply the biggest phony. She needed to go to church every weekend so she could be forgiven for all the harsh words and criticism she spewed about her colleagues during the week. The joke around the building was that the cross around her neck went into a spinning frenzy each time she stepped into a church. The sad part of it was that, just like Carly, she had no idea people saw right through her. Even the people who were so close to her occasionally spoke about her behind her back. Anytime you passed her in the hallway or ran into her in the faculty room, you would always get the biggest and phoniest hello that you could ever imagine. And you knew that as soon as you left the room, you would become the topic of conversation. Little did she know that others would rat her out at times. But it was never really addressed. Only a very small number of teachers are lucky enough to work in a district with zero tolerance for that behavior. In most places, it's simply ignored by administration.

When Corinne was the topic of conversation, Ariana would give her a call that evening to share the latest comments. Corinne spent weeks writing down what was said. But who would believe her? It was simply hearsay, words written down on paper. She knew she needed solid proof.

Both Anna and Alice knew where this story was going. Corinne pulled out her iPhone. "Are you ready?" she asked. Anna and Alice were starting to feel a bit uncomfortable, but also upset, angry, and sad for Corinne.

With a tap of a button, the sounds of venom oozed from the phone. It was appalling how these women had nothing better to do than rip a fellow colleague apart for no reason. Antionette was the worst. Meanwhile, most of the staff and administration knew that if you gave Antionette a test to identify states and countries or required her to demonstrate math skills above a third-grade level, there would be plenty of explaining to do for the parents.

And that is also a big problem within many districts. Most teachers are licensed to teach grades from nursery school through sixth grade. Yes, every teacher is allowed to have their grade preferences, but you're an educator. You should be able to teach any grade level because that's what your educational license states. But then again, it's usually best to keep certain teachers with a specific grade level for most of their career. It really wouldn't benefit students to put a kindergarten teacher in an intermediate grade when the teacher herself would struggle with some of the subjects she's supposed to be teaching, most notably math.

After about two minutes, Alice asked Corinne to turn it off. They had heard enough. Both Alice and Anna were filled with anger. They were all supposed to be professionals, but this group was not practicing what they preach to their students each day. "Hypocrite" should have been the word of the day in every classroom that morning.

Not that they needed to, but Anna and Alice apologized to Corinne and felt so sorry that she had to endure the evilness of the people she worked with. These are the same people who stand in front of their students each day and put on a show.

"I guess those self-esteem and empathy cards they're doing with their students don't apply to them," said Alice.

It's ironic how the district pays for programs to show students how to be empathetic and culturally conscious of their peers when the teachers need the programs as much or more so. Most young students come into school pure and honest. It's some of the educators who are the tainted ones.

Corinne was thankful to have the support of Alice and Anna. There was some relief for Corinne to have gotten it all out. While they were unlikely to get directly involved, she knew that the pair would guide her in the right direction. Sure enough, Anna and Alice both knew what Corinne should do, but they asked her what her plan was.

"I've made an appointment with Dr. Lee," said Corinne. She wasn't about to let this go. It was the "weird" girl's turn to put some people in their places, and she was going to enjoy every minute of it.

Corinne returned to her classroom. Anna and Alice hadn't been surprised by what they had heard. It was well-known throughout the building, by staff and even Dr. Lee, that certain teachers thought they had certain entitlements in their workplace. Close your door and do your thing was the best advice any teacher in education could be given. Mind your business, do your job, make the kids happy, and you should be happy. If anyone interferes with that, go after that person, and put a stop to it.

At a grade level meeting with Anna and Alice, Dr. Lee had once alluded to one of the members from hell, by stating, "There will always be people who wear God around their neck but have evil in their heart. You can't have it both ways, and if you do, you're a phony." Dr. Lee pulled no punches. You may have thought he wasn't aware of things, but he was. And if he didn't figure things out on his own, there was always a staff member who was more than happy to fill him in.

How the situation would be handled was anyone's guess, though. Sometimes the way things are handled in a school district is mind-boggling. Too often, administrators don't want to fix the problem.

Rather they avoid conflict at all costs. In their roundabout way, they might put out an email to the entire staff that very generally highlights a problem that has been brought to their attention. Meanwhile, it has nothing to do with 99 percent of the staff, and the one it should be targeting isn't self-aware enough to realize it. Even worse is when, instead of even trying to hit the target, administrators just join the game.

Sharon was once again on the money when she would complain about an email that had been sent out to all the teachers. You could hear her bellowing in the hallways, "Why can't they specifically tell the one staff member who didn't complete an assignment or hand in something by a given date? Why must we all question ourselves to make sure we did do what was asked of us? Which most of us already did. Talk to the person who didn't do their job. Don't waste all of our time with emails that don't apply to the majority of us."

Once again, Sharon knew exactly what she was talking about. Every moment of time when working with children is very precious. Stop wasting teachers' time with things that don't apply to them. If there's a specific teacher or teachers who didn't do something that was required of them, tell those teachers, not all of the staff, most of whom did do their jobs.

But now, hopefully, reckoning day was about to come. How it would be settled was anyone's guess.

DR. LEE, PLEASE CALL THE OFFICE

"Dr. Lee, please call the office." When staff heard that come over the loudspeaker, everyone was on alert. Dr. Lee was out of his office and may soon be stopping in to see you and your class. Most everyone liked Dr. Lee. He was fair, had a good sense of humor, and cultivated a great relationship with the kids.

Dr. Lee stood more than six feet three inches tall. His height made for great entertainment when he had to stand next to a kindergartner and reprimand them for their bad behavior. But he did it in his own special way. He had a hard time keeping a straight face when being serious about such a silly offense. He was one of those administrators who never bothered you. If you were doing your job, he felt no need to interfere. But do something that was totally ridiculous, and you would hear about it. “Run for the hills,” sixth grade teacher Jerry Schultz would joke and yell into your classroom when Dr. Lee was barreling down the hallway. This meant he was on a mission. When he stormed past without making any eye contact, you knew not to get in his way. Unfortunately, fourth grade teacher Kathy Rogers never understood that.

Kathy was a wonderful teacher. She did everything for her students. She worried about each and every one of them as if she had given birth to them herself. You could always see her waiting outside an extra thirty minutes after dismissal with a student who still needed to be picked up. The biggest question in that situation would be, “Doesn’t the parent know they have a child missing after school hours?” But that’s another story entirely.

Kathy needed constant approval. She was always questioning everything she did for her students. Dr. Lee never bothered her, but she bothered Dr. Lee. He demonstrated great patience for teachers like Kathy, but every once in a while, he was very blunt with his “Not now, Kathy!” He meant nothing by it, and she knew it. The whole building knew that Mrs. Rogers was an excellent teacher.

When Dr. Lee came up to heaven, you knew something was going on. He never liked climbing the stairs to the second floor if he didn’t have to. As he passed each classroom, heads covertly peeked out to see where he was heading. The odds-on favorite was Sharon’s room. Though Sharon and Dr. Lee got along quite well, Sharon’s opinions sometimes had to be “discussed.”

You knew he was done when you would hear his bellowing voice talking to students walking to the bathroom or a whole class returning from a special trip. He always made sure to compliment how well a class was walking in the hallway and say hello to all the kids, by name. A dedicated principal knows each and every family in the building. Sadly, in many instances, it's the child who visits the principal's office who consumes most of the attention, while the quiet ones slip through their time unnoticed. But he knew as well as most good educators that those are the students you especially get to know.

Dr. Lee had been a teacher for many years before he became a principal. He'd taught both the primary and intermediate grades for years in another district, so he knew what it was like to be a teacher. And he never forgot it.

Courtney had a friend who taught in another district and was suffering with a brand-new principal. This new leader had only taught one grade for just a few years before becoming principal. Any smart committee, hopefully represented with some teachers, would pass on a candidate like that. But sometimes there's a candidate who already has the job before they even get to the interview, unbeknownst to many of the committee members. It happens way too often. Ever wonder how that person got the job over someone else who was better qualified? The person who's dedicated themselves to the district for years gets screwed in the end. Yes, we all know the answer to that one.

The good thing about Dr. Lee was he did his best to make everything as fair as possible. He was a million times better than Dr. Andrews, the previous principal. When she left, they had a big celebration. She'd thought the party was for her, but everyone else knew it was really for the staff who didn't have to put up with her anymore.

For the entire staff, other than Anna and Alice, Dr. Andrews had kept everyone on edge. Anna and Alice backed each other up, so it was always two against one when there was any confrontation, which Anna and Alice never had to be concerned about. Deep down the staff knew Dr. Andrews had no idea what she was doing. She could never make a decision on her own. And when she did, it was usually a big mistake. Her biggest of blunders would spread like wildfire throughout the district, and she'd find a way to pin the mistake on her staff. The teachers avoided her as much as possible. When they did have to go to her for something, they took a deep breath and jumped in. But most of the time she wasn't even available. The staff were always told that she was in a meeting. It was the easy way out, because she didn't want to see staff either, unless she needed something from them.

Dr. Andrews was notorious for having a "12:30 meeting" every other Friday. If you happened to be passing by her office around 2:00 p.m. and were lucky enough to get a quick look, there was Dr. Andrews with a brand-new hairdo. She would sneak back in and stay in her office until the staff left on Friday afternoon. Once in a while something would bring her out of her office and everyone pretended that her hair wasn't different than it had been two hours ago. "What a joke!" Sharon would say.

Dr. Andrews lasted five long years before deciding to move on to a different administration position elsewhere. Being a principal wasn't her thing. She was a poor communicator. She didn't know how to talk to children, and most importantly, she didn't know how to talk civilly with the staff. Educators are quite lucky if they can get through their entire career without working with someone like Dr. Andrews.

Her biggest problem, which is what brought on her demise, was *always* taking the side of the parents. While parents often have very valid concerns for their children, Dr. Andrews *never* asked the teacher for their version of the story or investigated the claim before immediately agreeing with the parent. Nine times out of ten, there was plenty of backpedaling when the entire story came out, and the superintendent and the union often had to get involved. How a person with such poor people skills could be hired as principal—and even more baffling, receive tenure—just shows what a poor job some districts do when it comes to hiring. Dr. Andrews was another perfect example of someone who had gotten the job before she even walked into the interview.

"Dr. Lee, please call the office," came booming over the loudspeaker once again. He decided to stop in Courtney's room to use her phone.

Courtney had her entire class sitting on the classroom carpet, where she was doing a read-aloud for her students. She was quite skilled at doing voices for every character in a book. Each character had its own persona and voice, and the kids were eating it up. She was one of those teachers who created the memories all of her students would treasure. When one thinks back to a favorite childhood teacher, it's usually one who taught "outside of the box."

"Apparently, Corinne would like to see me," he said. As he left Courtney's room, she figured it had something to do with Corinne's visit to Anna and Alice's room earlier in the day. Even though she had nothing to do with Corinne's situation, her stomach began to churn. Courtney never liked disagreements. She wanted everyone to get along and be happy. The old movie *Pollyanna,* starring Hayley Mills, was one of her favorites. Knowing that was one of the crucial puzzle pieces to understanding who Courtney Reynolds really was.

SAME SHIT, DIFFERENT PLAYERS

When people say, "things never change," they're usually correct. Even when you feel sure something will improve, the same old situations usually continue.

Teachers are sometimes hopeful that when new administration comes in they will change the things in the district that are so ridiculous—maybe they will finally address the staff members who take advantage of things or bring down morale. That's always the hope. You're just waiting for a staff member to get their just deserts. Somewhere down the line, surely it has to happen, if there's a God in the world.

Margaret Evans taught fifth grade, just like Anna and Alice. Margaret did her own thing, which was just fine with Anna and Alice. It was just the way it was. Some of the teachers in heaven felt she would be best suited downstairs on the first floor, as she was always in everyone else's business instead of minding her own. She was notorious for making up stories and then telling others she'd heard it from someone else. Sharon had no problem correcting her when this would happen, much to the amusement of those who got to witness it.

The biggest problem with Margaret was that she was late for school every day. Not just once in a while, *every single day*. She always made the time to stop and pick up her large coffee, so who cares if she was twenty-plus minutes late. Who cares that everyone else followed the rules? Remember, there are no rewards for following the rules. She thought she was fooling people by not walking in the main door. She would sneak in through other entrances on these late mornings. Wasn't she aware that everyone knew she was late? Didn't she know she was the topic of conversation? She would deliberately leave her schoolbag and belongings downstairs and have one of her students retrieve it. Better to see a ten-year-old carrying those items than the person who is twenty to thirty minutes late for work. Once again, everyone knew what she was doing. The most ridiculous part was that she lived just ten minutes from work. There were other employees who had an hour-long drive each morning, and they would always arrive on time—usually early, in fact. Most people felt that Margaret's tardiness showed no respect for rules or the profession. All workers, not just teachers, have a responsibility. Some people don't have someone waiting for them when they arrive at their job, but teachers have at least twenty little ones sitting outside their door waiting patiently for them.

Most likely another reason for her habitual lateness was that Margaret *loved* to shop. She always did some grocery shopping before work, as well. Her biggest love was shopping online. Unfortunately, most of this was done while the kids worked at their desks. This was especially prevalent when the holidays were soon approaching. Some years, she would even ask her students, who were around the same age as her own kids at those times, what they thought of certain products for gifts. Actually, she could have turned it into a good lesson on taking surveys or comparing and contrasting various items. But her only thought was that she had shopping to do.

"Mrs. Evans, please call the office," echoed throughout the hallways. Being summoned over the PA system usually meant something was up. It usually meant you weren't where you were supposed to be. In this case she was in her classroom. The secretary was used to summoning her over the loudspeaker each morning, per Dr. Lee's request, just to let everyone know she was once again late for work.

Mrs. Evans quickly called the office and was told Dr. Lee would like to see her. She saw that it was Mia's prep period and asked if she could watch her class for a moment. As students continued on with their long division, Margaret headed to the main office.

As Margaret descended the stairwell, she could hear Dr. Lee bellowing, "Look at all of this!" She wondered what he was yelling about. She had no idea it would have anything to do with her. For once she hadn't been late that morning (miracles do happen!). As she entered, she caught the wide-eyed expression on the secretary's face. This was not a good sign. When Mrs. Baker gave you that look as you entered the office, you knew something was going on.

Mrs. Baker told Margaret to take a seat for a second as Dr. Lee needed to return a phone call ASAP. Mrs. Baker and Margaret made idle chitchat. During the conversation Margaret was hoping that Mrs.

Baker would give her a clue as to what was going on. Why had she been called to the office? Margaret could hear Dr. Lee on the phone behind his closed door. Her stomach began to feel tense and nervous. She could hear that his conversation was coming to an end. When the secretary saw he was off the phone, she buzzed him to say Margaret was waiting.

Margaret could hear him stand up from his chair and walk to his door. She gazed at the doorknob as it slowly turned. He opened the door and asked her in. Margaret noticed a smile on his face, which she was glad to see. Dr. Lee was known to occasionally get staff all riled up over something that was basically nothing. When he first started as their principal, he'd been notorious for emailing staff members over the weekend and asking to see them on Monday to "discuss something." You would think an administrator would know better than to do that over the weekend. Most people would be sick to their stomach, ruining their weekend by stressing over what he wanted. Nine times out of ten, it was nothing. His weekend emails soon subsided thanks to union representatives telling him he was upsetting his staff. So maybe she was overreacting to being called down to the office?

But then again, she had been called down in the middle of working with her students.

Dr. Lee had a very large office—the largest in the district, in fact. It was the size of a small classroom. You could probably fit fifteen children's desks in the room. He was the envy of other administrators whose offices were referred to as a "size-twelve shoebox."

While Dr. Lee was asking Margaret how she was and how the kids were, she observed the packages all around his office. This was nothing unusual. He often stored boxes of materials and workbooks there to be easily accessible when teachers needed something for their students. As long as his door was open and he wasn't in a meeting, teachers were welcome to come in and take what they need for their students. If he had it, it was yours.

As Margaret returned the question, asking about his family, she noticed that many of the boxes closest to Dr. Lee's desk said Amazon on them. She thought that was strange, as she was quite familiar with the names of all the publishing companies the district dealt with.

As Dr. Lee spoke about one of his college-bound sons, Margaret noticed a few items on Dr. Lee's big, solid wood desk. She noticed an opened box containing a new DVD player, a few books that were clearly not textbooks—including an unauthorized biography of Lady Gaga—and a bunch of boots in various colors. For a brief second, she thought these were some very odd items to be on Dr. Lee's desk. Did he wear those boots on the weekend? She tried to stay tuned in as he continued to babble on about all his kids, while he was moving the items around on his desk.

All of a sudden, Mrs. Evans felt an electric shock flow through her body. She started to feel weak and instant nausea came over her. She had just realized why she'd been summoned to the office.

Dr. Lee said, "Margaret, I apologize, but some of these boxes were opened by mistake by one of our aides." He explained that the aide thought they held some textbooks the sixth-grade teachers had been waiting for. He told the aide that the district doesn't order textbooks through Amazon.

Margaret didn't know what to say. She had been found out. While many of her colleagues knew she did her shopping on Amazon sometimes during the day, they never thought she wouldn't be careful to make sure the items were shipped to her home and not to her place of work.

The biggest kick in the gut were the packaging slips. Dr. Lee wasn't going to make a big deal of an address mistake, but he *was* going to make something of the date, day, and time that the orders were placed.

While looking at a wall calendar, Dr. Lee asked Margaret, "What time does your class have gym on Wednesdays?"

"At one thirty," she replied, feeling like her stomach had dropped into her toes.

He also asked what time fifth grade had lunch. She knew he already knew the answer to that question, since he was the one who made the lunch schedule.

Margaret knew there was no way out of this. Without even discussing it, he told Mrs. Baker to summon the custodian, because Mrs. Evans would need assistance with putting boxes into her car. Margaret left the office, with Mrs. Baker's eyes opened wider than ever.

After Max, the custodian, helped Margaret to her car, she returned to her classroom. She thanked Mia for watching her class. Mia wasn't so happy. In her mind, she had just spent her entire prep period watching another teacher's class instead of getting things ready for her own students.

While Sharon was escorting her students back to class, she noticed the interaction between Mia and Margaret. "I couldn't find you during your prep; where were you?" Sharon asked.

"I had to watch Margaret's class," Mia replied.

Sharon's eyes opened wide. Like everyone, Sharon heard that Margaret was summoned to the office to see Dr. Lee. As Sharon passed Courtney's class, she popped her head in and exclaimed, "Get ready for an email about something "we" shouldn't be doing."

Sure enough, at 2:50 pm, the email came out:

> Dear Staff,
> Please be advised that shopping online for personal items during the school day is prohibited. If you are shopping for school-related items, it should be done during your prep or lunch hour. Thank you for your cooperation.
> Sincerely,
> Dr. Lee

By the 3:00 p.m. dismissal, most staff members had seen the email and were giving each other the eye. It's the eye that says you all know something is going on. Once again an email had unnecessarily looped everyone in. Sharon would have preferred this email instead:

> Dear Staff,
> Today it was brought to my attention that your colleague, Mrs. Margaret Evans, has been doing online shopping during school hours. Please scowl at her while you pass her in the hallway so she knows never to do this again, and I don't have to involve the whole school staff.
> Sincerely,
> Dr. Lee

Like most teachers across the country, they all wish it was done Sharon's way.

ENOUGH IS ENOUGH

Dr. Lee finally found time to sit down and talk with Corinne. This kind of delay was quite common. You can schedule an appointment, but sometimes it's just not going to work out. It all depends on who's in charge. There are those who can juggle it all, and each day runs quite smoothly. Then there are the people who get rattled over every little thing. While some can handle just about any situation in ten minutes or less, others like to rehash the whole thing multiple ways, and it turns into an unproductive, hour-long discussion. Get in and get out; that is the way to handle things. Everyone knows that someone who just needs to repeat the obvious numerous times. Once again, there's no time to waste. Every moment that's wasted means less time for the children. Most things that come up in an elementary school aren't that serious. They can and should be handled quickly so that every other minor "emergency" can also be addressed quickly as it arises.

Even though she was feeling nervous, Corinne was glad to finally get the opportunity to tell Dr. Lee what was happening and why she was there. Her biggest concern was what would happen—if *anything* would—once she provided the evidence. This was cut and dry. This wasn't hearsay. This wasn't speculation. This wasn't behind-closed-doors gossip. This was a teacher who wanted to prove her case and had the ammunition to do so.

"So what brings you here today, Corinne?" Dr. Lee asked. He could tell that she was nervous. She was shifting in her seat, and her voice was a low and crackling when she began to speak.

Corinne laid it all on the table. The moment Dr. Lee asked if she was sure this was really going on, Corinne played the audio on her cell phone.

Dr. Lee took copious notes. Corinne could see he was writing staff members names down on a piece of paper with a little dash next to their name. He would write a few key words he heard from the audio after their name. After listening for about three minutes, it was enough.

Dr. Lee looked over what he had jotted down and took a long pause. He profusely apologized to Corinne. He wished she had come to him sooner. She said she was waiting for the evidence. He inquired as to how she had gotten the audio of the staff's vitriol towards her. She told him she preferred not to say. She knew Alice and Anna would take that information to their grave. She told Dr. Lee she knew recording someone without them knowing shouldn't be done but had no plans to play it for anyone else. She didn't mention that Alice and Anna had been the first to hear it.

She did it because there could be no misunderstandings, no

denying this was happening.

Dr. Lee asked how Corinne would like to proceed. She was honest and said she had no idea. She would like it to just stop. Dr. Lee said that he needed to bring it to the attention of the superintendent. He would try not mention names, and maybe they could brainstorm how to put an end to this destructive internal bullying. He assured her this would all be resolved. It may take some time, but it would be taken care of. He advised that she not play the audio on her phone to anyone. She said from this moment on, no one else would hear it, which was the truth. Corinne left the office to a once again wide-eyed expression from Mrs. Baker.

Mrs. Baker had been a secretary in the district for more than twenty years. She was a kind woman and very helpful to the staff. But she was always befuddled if she had more than one thing to do at a time. She would lose total concentration if someone entered the office while she was on the phone. It was always best to stand by the door and wait to be waved in. That scenario meant you would have her full attention. If she was in the middle of a conversation with you and the phone rang, she would let it go to voicemail. Each call and each walk-in would be taken very seriously no matter what the situation or question was. Mrs. Baker loved all the staff members and got along with everyone. Everyone except Dr. Andrews. When Dr. Andrews announced she was moving on, Mrs. Baker was no doubt the happiest person on the entire staff and probably in the whole school district. She was tired of glossing over every misstep Dr. Andrews took over the five years she was there. She was tired of always covering for her, telling people that she was in a meeting when in fact she was in her office with the door closed, chatting with her friends on school time.

Mrs. Baker had contemplated leaving at least a dozen times over the five years Dr. Andrews was in charge. Her husband encouraged her to do it all the time. Most guessed he was tired of hearing his wife complain each night at the dinner table. But she did have two children who would be going to college in the near future, and every little bit of money would help. Not that she was making good money. She would often say to sympathetic ears, "Look where I work. You think I'm making the big bucks?" So for the most part, she put up with the daily stresses of working with Dr. Andrews. But there was one day that almost sent Mrs. Baker out the door.

Despite her need to deal with one situation at a time, Mrs. Baker was the most organized individual around. Everything was done efficiently, and she was on top of everything. She remembered all conversations. Staff would joke that she had a little notebook in her desk with transcripts of every conversation she'd had in her entire life. Thanks to her impeccable memory, there was no doubt that Mrs. Baker would win this office showdown with Dr. Andrews.

It was a Friday afternoon when Ms. Hochman entered the main office. She saw she had made good eye contact with Mrs. Baker and knew she had her full attention. Ms. Hochman was the music teacher. She was there to retrieve the funds she had collected to purchase instruments for her students.

"I'm here for the money for the school recorders," she said. "I'm picking them up tomorrow from the music store." Mrs. Baker quickly headed for the safe. Any collections that were made were always put there. Ms. Hochman could hear Mrs. Baker mumbling to herself as she was rustling through the numerous envelopes that were kept inside.

Mrs. Baker returned to her desk and told Ms. Hochman that her envelope was not in the safe. She told Mrs. Baker that she had handed it in, and Mrs. Baker knew she was correct.

Thinking back to that day, Mrs. Baker remembered taking the envelope from Ms. Hochman. As she entered Dr. Andrews office to open the safe, she was waved away. Mrs. Baker knew Dr. Andrews was on one of those "very important calls" with one of her friends. Most likely they were making their weekend plans. Dr. Andrews grabbed the envelope and whispered that she would put it in the safe. *Does she even know the combination?* Mrs. Baker wondered. She didn't recall ever seeing Dr. Andrews open the safe.

Mrs. Baker told Ms. Hochman the story of that day and said she would talk to Dr. Andrews as soon as she was back from her meeting. This was basically code for when her color, rinse, and blow-dry at the beauty parlor was finished. After all, it was Friday afternoon.

As the minutes slowly ticked by, Mrs. Baker became more and more nervous about how this story would play out. From past experience she was quite used to Dr. Andrews passing the blame for all of her blunders. Mrs. Baker was definitely not having this, especially when it dealt with school funds.

Mrs. Baker tried to concentrate on her work the best she could. It was not the way she wanted to end the school week. Friday was supposed to be the day to tidy up loose ends and cherish the fact that there would be two glorious days off from work. This latest problem needed to be solved now and not ruin the weekend.

With her office door open, Mrs. Baker could hear Dr. Andrews talking with a staff member in the hallway. By now Mrs. Baker was at the boiling point.

Dr. Andrews entered the main office with her usual line.

"Everything good?" she would ask.

"Not today," replied Mrs. Baker. Mrs. Baker explained that Ms. Hochman had come to retrieve the recorder money so she could pick the instruments up on Saturday, which when you think about it, was on her own time. Mrs. Baker told Dr. Andrews that the envelope was not in the safe.

Dr. Andrews quickly told Mrs. Baker to look again because there were so many envelopes and papers in the safe, and it was probably just mixed in.

Mrs. Baker suggested they do it together. After going through the entire safe, it was obvious that the envelope was not there.

Dr. Andrews asked Mrs. Baker, "When did you put the envelope in the safe?"

"I didn't, you did," replied Mrs. Baker.

Mrs. Baker could see that Dr. Andrews did not like this response. "I have nothing to do with the music funds," Dr. Andrews said.

Without missing a beat, Mrs. Baker retold the entire story of Dr. Andrews taking the envelope from her and saying that she would put the envelope in the safe after her phone call.

For a split second Mrs. Baker could see that Dr. Andrews was about to go into her denial mode. She and the entire staff had seen that look way too many times. But this time would be different. Mrs. Baker's eyes were open wider than ever, and there was no way she was going to let Dr. Andrews pass the buck on this one.

"Well, it has to be here somewhere," Dr. Andrews nervously suggested. She quickly began rummaging through the piles of papers on her desk. It was apparent there were no large manila envelopes there. But when you're the cause of the problem, moving things around on your desk buys you a few seconds.

It was now three o'clock in the afternoon. Classes were being dismissed, and teachers were heading to the parking lot. The weekend had arrived, but not for Dr. Andrews and Mrs. Baker. Ms. Hochman came to the office hoping to retrieve the envelope. Mrs. Baker popped her head out, eyes wide open and whispered that she would have to wait until Monday. By the look on Mrs. Baker's face, Ms. Hochman knew it was time to hightail it out of there.

Dr. Andrews suggested that it would have to wait until Monday to resolve this latest problem. The usually mild-mannered Mrs. Baker was not having it. Mrs. Baker knew this would give Dr. Andrews an entire weekend to spin this story, and the blame would fall upon her.

"Unless you threw it out by mistake, it's here," Mrs. Baker said sternly. We're not leaving until we search this entire office." Dr. Andrews knew that Mrs. Baker meant business.

They attacked all parts of the room. Drawers, windowsill, and closet. Dr. Andrews grabbed a pack of interoffice envelopes she kept in the bottom of her desk drawer. These were the envelopes that were used to send mail throughout the district. She must have had about 50 of them stuffed in her drawer. Sure enough, after rummaging through about twenty five of them, there it was, all mixed in. A sense of relief washed over Mrs. Baker. Dr. Andrews handed the money to Mrs. Baker, who quickly put it in the safe. There would be no waiting for an apology because it wasn't coming. Mrs. Baker returned to her desk, to finish up her day's work. In a matter of two minutes, Dr. Andrews said her usual, "have a good weekend," and left the office. Mrs. Baker was in no mood to reply, "You, too."

So the day Dr. Andrews said she was leaving for better

opportunities, Mrs. Baker felt like a free woman again. Depending on her mood, once in a while Mrs. Baker will share one of her many stories about Dr. Andrews. It usually happens at a morning breakfast or the yearly holiday party. Those who worked with Dr. Andrews would relish hearing the stories. The running joke was, "Someone get Mrs. Baker a drink and then gather round."

MEETINGS, ASSEMBLIES, AND NO SPECIALS . . . OH MY!

Courtney was prying open a can of paint. When the top popped off, she smiled at the beautiful color. It was a very light blue. Maybe even more of a sky blue. She took one of the wooden sticks and stirred it, then grabbed a brush to dip in the can. But the paint was not sticking to the brush. She found that very odd. After numerous attempts, she was finally able to cover the brush with paint. She stood up and walked over to one of the four walls that surrounded her. To her surprise, the paint wouldn't stick to the wall either. It dripped down from the brush onto her hand, but it wasn't adhering to the wall.

Suddenly she heard a loud dragging sound behind her. Turning, she saw a very tall blonde man dragging a ladder across the floor. She couldn't comprehend who this stranger was. She'd never seen him before. As she laid her brush down, she looked up, amazed at his height. Just as she was trying to get a closer look at his face, everything went dark.

At that moment, a piercing beeping sound began. Courtney opened one eye. She could see those dreaded three numbers and two letters, 4:46 a.m. It was time to get up and, worse, it was Monday.

Courtney jumped out of bed. She tried to be positive, even though a new week lay ahead. She loved her class, so that was the best, if not the only, reason to get up that day. Like Mrs. Baker, Courtney was very organized. Her clothes were laid out from the night before, her lunch was made, and the coffee maker just had to be plugged in. Courtney brought her own coffee to school each day. During the cold and flu season, or anything else the world had to offer, she didn't need anyone else touching her cup and serving her. In no time at all, she was hopping into her car and ready for another week. She loved listening to her favorite songs on her twenty-minute commute.

When she arrived at work, she basked in the quietness. There would always be one or two early birds already there and working. The others would arrive within the next hour.

Courtney liked to make sure each and every day would run smoothly. Every detail was important to her. Kids pick up on it very easily if a teacher is not prepared. With approximately five different subjects to teach each day, she believed the transition was very important.

This day would be an especially busy one. Not only did she have to teach, but she also had meetings to attend to discuss the progress of her students.

For Courtney, welcoming her class into the room each morning was a joy. Yes, some years were not that way, but for the most part Courtney truly enjoyed her pupils. She loved to give each student the opportunity to shine and allow them to express themselves. She would cringe any time she witnessed colleagues preventing students from being who they were. Yes, action was needed for those who were always disruptive, but she was very intentional about allowing space for a student who likes to talk and share their thoughts.

They would always remember her for that.

Courtney started the day knowing a portion of it would be covered by a substitute teacher so she could attend her meeting. Progress meetings were not a favorite of teachers, and their reasons were justified. Most meetings ran smoothly because most teachers were just going through the motions.

But teachers like Sharon wouldn't stand for any of the nonsense.

When Sharon would attend a class progress meeting, she was ready. She had copious notes, data, and a big chip on her shoulder, which was sometimes needed.

As Sharon would discuss her students, she was surrounded by various support teachers and administration. Occasionally, Sharon would look up and notice that many could care less about what she had to say. Remember, while most people liked her, a handful did not. Her brash, cut-to-the-chase attitude was not appreciated by everyone. Sharon didn't enjoy her time being wasted. "Let's get to it" was another of her favorite things to say.

After the run-down of her class, it was time to hear from the chuckle patch. With everyone rambling on, it reminded Sharon of the patch of flowers from the children's television show, *The Magic Garden*. The chuckle patch was a group of flowers that would move about and chatter all at the same time.

The suggestions from the chuckle patch were the same year after year. Sharon was always amazed by how one colleague had all the answers for her. The person told her just what to do for a student they never met and never worked with. While most of her colleagues would just shake their heads—the quickest way to bring a close to the meeting—Sharon would push right back at everything she disagreed with. Especially from someone who acted like they knew more than they really did. Sharon was open to new ideas and suggestions, but it was always the same things from the same people.

Every time, Sharon felt sorry for the new members of the chuckle patch. It was apparent that the elder chucklers had no interest in the newcomers' opinions. In fact, this was common in all aspects of the school. The staff agreed that administration needed to grow a pair and put a stop to the handful of people who consistently monopolized every meeting. Over the years, Sharon and her former colleagues had come to learn just why certain staff members seemed to have more power in a meeting than the administrator. (Refer to "shenanigans" in *Webster's Dictionary* for details.)

Despite the frustrations with these meetings, they all eventually came to an end. The teachers would return to their classes, and the chuckle patch would finally disperse until the next time. Everyone did what they had to do, and the best teachers continued to do everything possible to give their students all they needed to be successful.

When Courtney returned to her room, she didn't have much

time to get any work in. It was time for the monthly torture fest.

Mrs. Baker's voice came over the loudspeaker to invite all classes down for the morning assembly. These announcements were usually met with a loud groan, and not just from the teachers. Students, especially the older ones, knew that the monthly assemblies were a crapshoot. You just never knew what you were going to get. What sounded good on paper might not translate so well in front of four hundred students and a few dozen adults.

If they were lucky, it would be a breezy forty-five minutes of light entertainment. But most of the time it was forty-five minutes of cringeworthy moments. Even if you never saw or heard the speaker, you could always tell how an assembly was going by watching the faces of the fifth and sixth graders and the adults. The little ones were more easily entertained.

You had to give some credit to the performers who did this for a living. It couldn't be easy for them, especially the ones who traveled from state to state. At the end, the audience would always offer a round of applause, whether they liked it or not. The real reviews rolled in on the journey back to the classroom—or once the classroom door had closed behind them.

When Courtney and her class resumed their work, she had approximately forty minutes to squeeze in one more subject. Lunch and an afternoon special were on the horizon.

When teachers have a day or sometimes even a week of interruptions, which include assemblies, pull-outs, push-ins, and anything else that disrupts a "normal" day, the detailed plans that took a whole weekend to prepare become a good idea that doesn't happen.

You could always count on Sharon to exclaim that her plans for the week were pure "fiction." With all good intentions, if she was able to complete half of what she had planned for the week, she would feel accomplished.

While the kids were at lunch, Courtney would eat her daily salad in front of the computer and prepare for the afternoon. She never ventured into the faculty room to eat. Especially now with the sense that something was going on in the building, that was the last place she wanted to be. She knew Alice and Anna ate together each day, planning lessons and talking about what they'd watched over the weekend.

On this particular Monday, Mrs. Baker took a break from her lunch to announce over the speaker that there would be no afternoon specials.

Courtney could hear groans and a couple of bad words emanate from some of the teachers. Courtney didn't mind so much. She loved her class, and it gave her an opportunity to get more work done. But she did sympathize with the other teachers. A prep period gave teachers more time to plan, prepare for the next day, or just get a break from their class. If you had a group of students that could turn your hair grey, your prep period meant everything to you. Worst of all, this was happening on a Monday with an afterschool meeting still to come. This was not the way a new school week should begin.

But sadly, it was nothing new.

By the time the school day ended, teachers and students would both be exhausted. For most students it was time to go home. For the staff it was time for meetings. Meetings on a Monday were always tough. It was a terrible idea to start off the week by exhausting the entire staff who still had four more days to go.

Alice and Anna, the school veterans, much preferred the days of yesteryear. Every week they used to have a one-hour midweek meeting. Some would last an hour, and if there wasn't much to report or go over, they would end early. No one wanted to waste everyone's time.

The way things were now just gave Sharon more fuel to add to the fire. You could always hear her saying, "What's the point of all these meetings? They're never beneficial. They're just for show. Look at us. We have a meeting for this, a meeting for that. Just let the teachers teach. Stop wasting our time."

It wasn't only Sharon who felt this way. Alice and Anna understood the real reason for the meetings. It was just a handful of teachers who needed to keep busy or be reminded of things. Most staff members were workhorses, but there would always be those few who weren't working at their full capacity.

It's the same as when an entire class gets punished because of the few who caused the problem. These days, some parents flip out if that happens, as perhaps they should when their obedient child has to suffer the consequences that really should apply just to a few others. Administration would agree that's not how you ought to handle a situation. It's too bad they don't really practice what they preach when it comes to their staff.

Courtney trudged down the stairs with two bags filled with books and papers. She headed out to her car to get ready for the long drive home. Although she only lived twenty minutes from the school, she could count on close to forty-five minutes when she headed home during rush hour. She usually didn't mind. She loved listening to her classic tunes. Her favorite oldies would keep her company for the ride home. Courtney always tried to stay focused on her drive while heading home, but her mind was always on the next school day. There were times when Courtney would be waiting at a traffic light and wonder when she'd passed the supermarket she'd wanted to stop at on the way home.

When Courtney arrived at her house, it was a typical evening. She would make herself some dinner, then go through her mail and pay any bills, if needed. She tried to refrain from making any phone calls on Monday nights as she liked to get to bed a little extra early at the beginning of the week.

As Courtney pulled the covers over her, she imagined what her life would be like in the upcoming year. *When will Mr. Right arrive? Will he* ever *arrive?* She wondered for the hundredth time if she should get a pet. But who would watch it while she was at work? All these thoughts rolled around in her head. It wasn't a good idea to get too focused on any particular dream or problem when one is trying to fall asleep. Tomorrow was another day. Her students were her main priority. Any other nonsense that cluttered the halls that surrounded her was something she had no time for.

OH, THE WEATHER INSIDE IS FRIGHTFUL

As fast as summer ended and school began, fall flitted by at breakneck speed and before anyone knew it, it was time to pull out that ugly Christmas sweater. The week before the extended holiday vacation always seemed to creep up faster than should have been possible. For educators, the goal was simply to make it through the week. Those with any experience knew they wouldn't get to all the work they'd planned, and that was alright. Kids get so excited about the upcoming festivities, that it's just not the best idea to start teaching fractions the week before Christmas.

Sharon would try to start the week off as calmly as possible. She was a pro at this and knew the calmer she was, the calmer her students would be. On Monday, she would act like it was just an ordinary week. She would keep to the daily routine, and all the work would get done. While some teachers may ease up on homework that particular week, Sharon thought otherwise. She believed if she started off any week—especially a pre-holiday week—differently, then by Wednesday she would have completely lost her students for the remaining days.

This week also gave administrators time to tie up any remaining loose ends with staff and parents. Dr. Lee believed in starting off the new year with a clean slate.

As quiet as the administrators believed they were with their behind-closed-doors goings on and perpetual drama, most staff were usually well aware of the things they weren't supposed to know about.

Sharon had a feeling that something was up with Corinne over the past few weeks. An occasional "hello" or "how are the kids?" was the extent of their usual interaction. But the week before Christmas inspired more conversation among staff members. Most of them were in the same boat. They still had holiday shopping to do, and many were preparing their holidays menus. Anyone listening in might overhear various teachers swapping traditional recipes with each other. Some were also talking about the traveling they would be doing over the holidays. Hearing about travel plans was a great indicator that some of the staff would be missing in action on the last day before break.

As the week trudged on, the wear on each person's face was apparent. They just had to make it to Friday and the finish line. And in reality, Thursday was the last day for getting any kind of work done. The last day before holiday vacation is meant to be pure fun. These are the days students remember the most.

On the second to last day before the holiday break, most of the teachers would gather at a local restaurant after work. It was a time to have a drink, nibble on an appetizer, and unwind. It also gave some staff the opportunity to catch up with colleagues they rarely got to see during the school day. Though when Alice and Anna looked around the bar, they noted that staff usually kept to the same group they interacted with at the school.

"Heaven forbid they spend a few minutes with any other colleagues!" Sharon would say.

Alice and Anna would each order a pinot grigio, and that one glass would last them the two hours for which they would partake in this holiday fare. They were always good at keeping tabs on who was into their third drink and giving each other the eye.

Sharon joined Alice and Anna at their table. "Where's Mia?" asked Sharon.

Courtney overheard as she approached the table, and she responded, "She wasn't feeling well and went straight home."

As the four of them chatted away, Anna and Alice could see Corinne standing around looking unsure of herself with her usual ginger ale in hand. Alice waved her over, and Corinne pulled up a chair to join them. Their conversation was centered around their holiday plans. Occasionally they would turn their heads when a roar of sound would come from their fellow colleagues. This would automatically raise the eyebrows of a few of them.

Now that Corinne had joined them, Alice and Anna were hoping they would learn what had come of her talk with Dr. Lee. They knew she wouldn't bring it up in front of Courtney and especially not Sharon.

They couldn't have planned it any better when two waiters

brought out the trays of food and placed them down at the other end of the bar. Sharon asked Courtney if she wanted to go and take inventory of what was being set out. They would no doubt return with a report of the tasty morsels that were on offer.

As soon as they were out of earshot, Corinne leaned in. "I never filled the two of you in about my meeting with Dr. Lee," she whispered to Alice and Anna.

"When did you get to speak to him?" Alice asked. It had been weeks since Corinne had played her infamous phone recording for them, and they'd never heard what had come of it.

Corinne explained that Dr. Lee had made the superintendent aware of the situation. Corinne added that she didn't want to make it into a big thing. She just wanted to make sure the administration was well aware of how specific staff members treated each other in a place where children are being taught. A place where the adults are supposed to be the role models.

As Corinne looked around, she had the satisfaction of knowing that the higher-ups were all aware of what was behind the big smiles of some of their employees, and what they were capable of saying about a fellow colleague.

As usual Sharon returned to the table with plates filled with food. One thing you could say about Sharon: she always made sure everyone was taken care of.

"What are we going to do with all this food, Sharon?" asked Anna.

"We're going to eat it!" she replied. Courtney passed around plates, napkins, and forks to all of them. It was time to kick off the long vacation. Sure, they had to go in and "teach" for one more day, but in reality, the break had begun. With a gleam in her eye, Corinne raised her glass of ginger ale. “Happy New Year!” she exclaimed, to a round of clinking glasses.

MAMA MIA

There was no need for an alarm this morning. Courtney had twisted and turned all night long. She knew she wasn't alone. Most of America's teachers hadn't gotten the best sleep that night. Across the country, teachers had just enjoyed approximately ten days off. It was a time of celebrating, entertaining, going out, and being with family. But as fun as it is, it's really not a vacation. It's pure exhaustion. To make it worse, many schools reopen the day after New Year's Day. This cruelty can't even be explained. If you want to see family on New Year's Day, you can't really enjoy it with the next day's work looming in the back of your mind. It's amusing how districts promote family togetherness, and then they open school the day after New Year's Day when families across the country are gathering together, many of them visiting relatives in other states.

Walking into school the morning after the holidays, everything feels a little slower and a whole lot quieter than usual. Being a planner, Courtney, had made sure before she left for vacation that her first day back was already set up.

As she walked down the hallway, she could see Alice and Anna were already in. There they sat with their cups of coffee, planning what they wanted to accomplish for the day. They waved Courtney in when she peeked in through the door. Their first order of business was to let her know there was no need for her to go down and make copies. The copier still wasn't fixed. The machine had broken two weeks before vacation. This was another appropriate complaint from the staff. When more than fifty people are using the same machine each day, it's bound to break down. God forbid someone in power might think to put two machines into the building where teachers invested their time and energy into the students. You'd think this simple way to support student success would be important enough to the district.

Now that copying couldn't be done, Courtney sat for a moment to chat with Anna and Alice. "Is Mia in yet?" asked Anna.

Courtney told them Mia still wasn't feeling well and wasn't coming in.

"That's not good; what's wrong with her?" asked Alice.

Courtney said it would probably be best if Mia explained when she returned.

A line like that was quite common in a work atmosphere. Either you were allowed to know what was going on, or you weren't. It was amazing how some people were made privy to things related to a fellow colleague and some were not. As Sharon would say, "It's usually some idiot who makes up those rules."

Anna and Alice were not ready to accept Courtney's response.

They weren't going to be outsiders. No, they weren't going to tempt Courtney to break any promises to Mia, but they would figure it out without Courtney getting into trouble.

All they wanted to know was whether Mia had seen a doctor and if she would recover from this "illness." Courtney told them that yes, she had, and there's nothing to worry about.

"So when is she due?" Anna asked.

Courtney's lips quirked up into a smile. You couldn't fool Anna and Alice. They've seen it all over the years. Courtney said that when Mia returns, they can ask her anything they want. Courtney excused herself. It was time to go type up an activity she had planned to copy for her students. In about thirty minutes, the sound of classroom printers would be singing in harmony.

When Courtney left, Alice and Anna looked at each other. They knew what would happen over the next few weeks and months. When a nontenured teacher of two years wasn't married and had a baby on the way, there would be a buzz in the air, especially once she started to show. For Alice and Anna, it would be their job to make sure that this young lady wouldn't have to put up with any whispers around the building or be spoken about in the way Corinne had been for years. They knew there was only one person who would lead the troops on this one.

A knock came at the door. It was Sharon. "So, how was everyone's holiday break?"

Mia took an entire week off before returning the second week of January. Those who cared to ask about her were told she was getting over the flu. The in-crowd in this situation was Courtney, Alice, Anna, Sharon, and Corinne. Corinne had a vested interest in protecting Mia. She would no longer be the doormat. Instead she would be the protector of others in need.

Mia did feel embarrassed, but her friends reassured her. She'd been with the same man for eight years. They just never had any interest in getting married. But now they were planning to wed in the near future.

Sharon, never one to keep an opinion to herself, thought a spring wedding would be nice.

On her first day back, Mia made an appointment with Dr. Lee. It was time to put it out there. When she walked into the office, wide-eyed Mrs. Baker was there. *Did she already know?* Mia wondered to herself. Mia knew she was starting to show, so maybe the cat was already out of the bag.

The meeting with Dr. Lee couldn't have gone smoother. He congratulated Mia and told her to simply ask for whatever she needed. If she needed some rest time during the day, he would get coverage for her. When she explained that her morning sickness was what had kept her home last week, he told her to feel free to arrive a little later in the morning, if needed.

The baby was scheduled to arrive in May, so there would be lots of planning to do. Mia told Dr. Lee that she'd decided to tell the staff when it came up. She wouldn't be knocking on everyone's classroom door, but she wasn't going to be hiding it. He agreed with her strategy and said he would bring it up at the next faculty meeting. Mia felt quite calm and at ease. This happened all the time. She was no different than other women. Life would go on, and she would be a mother within five months.

As the days and weeks went by, everyone was always asking Mia if she needed anything. Apparently, the news of the mother-to-be had brought a calm to the building. There was enough crap going on in the world; did it really need to be brought up in school as well? Most people felt that way. Most, that is, except for Vivian Kramer.

A DONKEY NAMED EEYORE IS HER NAME

Vivian Kramer raced down the hallway to her classroom each morning. She wasn't late by any means; this was just how she moved around the building. It was usually better to give her a quick wave than to exchange any words with her. In most cases, it was a mistake to start a conversation with her. She was a lovely person but always so gloomy. She never seemed happy and had a knack for finding the downside in any situation. She walked around with the weight of the world on her shoulders. Every once in a while, in a weak moment, someone would ask Vivian how she was, and that would be it. They were then trapped for twenty minutes listening to how everything in her life was going wrong.

No one could understand why. She had a good-looking,

hard-working husband. She had three children, all in their twenties, and they all seemed to have great lives. It was just something everyone had learned: that if Vivian wasn't complaining about something or wasn't feeling down in the dumps, that would be a sign that something was up. Everyone counted on her gloom, even as they avoided it.

Vivian could be a real grouch at times, and her students knew it. It was always best that she taught sixth grade. The older students could let her moods roll off their shoulders. The little ones wouldn't understand it. They would just see her as a cranky old lady. Not that some of the sixth graders didn't feel that way, too.

At the same time, she was a world history fanatic and a super teacher when it came to teaching that topic. In education, you didn't have to be an expert in every area, but many teachers were specifically known for their strong suits in specific curriculum areas.

Despite being a gloomy old Eeyore, the sad jackass from the Winnie the Pooh series, she was very happy for other people's successes. When it was revealed that Mia was expecting at the last faculty meeting, Vivian was already planning the shower with Courtney. Vivian believed when you plan something, you should do it right or not do it at all.

Although the baby shower was going to be a surprise for Mia, she knew it was coming. Baby showers and wedding showers were the norm, so she quietly expected it. The only surprise would be when.

At two months until the celebration, Vivian began planning in earnest. Things like this gave her purpose. She would talk about it every day up until the occasion, and these events seemed to be one of the only things that consistently lifted Vivian's spirits. But when she was down, she was down.

Many said Vivian was depressed because she deprived herself of basic nutrition. She was tall and pencil thin. Whenever you saw her eating, which was a rarity, it usually consisted of two whole wheat crackers, a wedge of cheese, and black coffee. That kind of daily diet would make almost anyone grumpy. When the fall winds were whipping around, you could see Vivian struggling not to be blown away by the gusts as she made her way in from the parking lot. But despite all of that, she was in school every morning on time and ready to teach.

Schools are made up of a cast of characters. Each and every person brings something unique. Anyone, anywhere who has teacher friends will recognize at least most of these characters. They exist everywhere.

But the months were flying by, and June, the finish line, would be here before anyone knew it. There was plenty to do before then.

WHAT'S BEST FOR CHILDREN?

Why do teachers teach? That's a question every educator should be asked each year on the first day of school. Maybe it can be incorporated into the string of first day, back-to-school activities for teachers. It might be more beneficial than sitting for ninety minutes listening to some yahoo whose name will be forgotten within the week. Maybe administrators could pass out index cards and propose that question. It could even be anonymous, if that's what teachers preferred. Either way, it would undoubtedly inspire some good dialogue among staff.

But no, we'll spend hours talking about the new reading and writing series the district has just purchased all while wondering, *Didn't we just have a new one three years ago?*

But this question should be pondered every year. As time passes, it would be interesting to see how educators' responses change. They shouldn't be saying the same thing year after year. An initial response will usually be something like, "I like kids," or, "I want to mold the future," or, "It's what I'm good at." Unfortunately, these common responses just don't cut it anymore. If this is what one has decided to dedicate their lives to, their answer to the question of *why* needs to reflect a more specific and personal passion about teaching.

Senior teaching staff have watched so much change over the decades. As exciting as it is to see the passion in new educators, it's just as disheartening when you see that passion dissipate over the years. Unfortunately, these feelings seem to be hitting teachers younger and younger.

As in many jobs, after doing the same thing for twenty years, burnout is quite common among teachers. When an individual recognizes it in themselves, they search for ways to reignite their passions and reinvent themselves for the job they once loved. So what's causing these feelings? Why are many new teachers yearning to try a different career after only around five years of teaching?

Most of their reasons, both recognized and subconscious, stem from the top. Too often, educators are put into higher positions they are not qualified for. For some, it's just to have a new title. Some of them don't know how to listen. They don't value the opinions of the people who are on the frontlines each and every day teaching children. Never put anyone in authority who hasn't been a classroom teacher for at least a few years. And more specifically, an elementary school teacher.

Sharon came up the stairs with her class and passed Anna's room. When Sharon had something to say to another teacher, and her students were around, she would motion for them to walk ahead and tell them to wait at the classroom door for her. This would give her about thirty seconds to pass on a word or two to one of her colleagues. Today, it was Anna who would get an earful in about thirty seconds. Many felt Sharon would be great on *The $100,000 Pyramid* game show because she would be able to answer all the questions correctly in just thirty seconds.

"What's going on?" Anna asked.

"I just heard the 'What's best for children?' line again," Sharon replied.

Anna instantly rolled her eyes. This saying, which is an important one, had turned into a cliché. A phrase that would get administrators out of being truthful, upfront, or honest.

And this is the reason why many teachers have become slowly disgusted over the years. They're tired of the taglines, the go-to words, and the good old standby phrases that have all become meaningless.

School districts should always be doing what's best for children, and most of them do their best to do so. There are so many caring and wonderful educators who dedicate their lives to children, and the world needs more of them. But it's those who don't maintain that level that are causing the walls of education to crumble around many educators.

As the end of a school year draws close, you can see that many teachers are getting anxious. As the paperwork becomes intense, for some, the biggest concern is what their position will be the following year. While some enjoy a change of grade level, for others it rocks their world—more than it really should. Most elementary school teachers are licensed for nursery school through sixth grade, so technically they should be ready for whatever may come their way.

There are always some teachers who never have to worry about a grade change. They will stay in the same grade level for their entire career. There are many reasons for this. In most cases, it's because the teacher is an expert at what they do. They provide a school year that is superior. Parents and students look forward to having that one teacher they've heard about for years when they get to that grade. It's a successful, productive school year, with a teacher who knows how to connect with all kinds of students. For a parent, there's nothing more stressful than when their child and their new teacher aren't a good fit. It makes going to school every single morning stressful for the entire year. If you have a quiet and meek student, they will not thrive with a teacher who tends to be high strung or domineering. So when you have that teacher who can provide a great environment for every student, you don't want to disrupt something that works so well.

But then, there are the teachers who are never moved and should be. It's sad when the entire staff sees it, but the administrator does not. In most cases it's just one of many examples of cronyism. When teachers get a little too close to an administrator, this can guarantee they won't be moved from their grade. Unless, of course, the teacher makes a specific request.

When teachers are rotated to a different grade, one of the reasons may be that the teacher hasn't revamped their lessons over the years. What they do may have worked years ago, but it's not cutting the mustard now. If the educator is able to identify what they need to work on, they should be given the opportunity to improve. If they don't, a change is needed.

Some teachers love change. Some, but not many. It gives an enthusiastic educator the opportunity to learn a different curriculum. The first year in a new grade can be a great learning experience, not only for the students but also for the teacher. It's a year of learning together with one's students.

Dr. Lee believed in movement. He believed teachers shouldn't be in a grade for more than five to seven years. Yes, he knew that some individuals were made for certain grades, and that's where he would keep them. The most nurturing kindergarten teacher who has huge successes each year and is loved by parents isn't going anywhere. That's one apple cart that should never be disrupted without a very compelling reason.

You would never move a sixth-grade teacher like Vivian Kramer to kindergarten, unless you wanted to see a bunch of depressed five-year-old children trudging through the hallways. If you're not going to display childlike qualities to your students, it's best to be in an upper grade.

The news that a teacher is going to be moved to a different grade can be delivered in numerous ways. It all depends on the administrator.

There's administrator "A" who comes to your door and says, "Hey, next year you're teaching fifth grade instead of third." Those are the administrators most educators love. They're quick and to the point. There's no big lead up, and no drama. Most educators appreciate that type of delivery. Usually, the response is simply, "Oh, okay!" And the day continues for everyone.

Then there's administrator "B." They live for this day. They make every teacher walk down to the office to learn their fate for the next school year. This is juvenile, ridiculous, and disrespectful to fellow educators. A teacher would be severely reprimanded if these tactics were applied to students in their classroom. But this is typical with administrator "B." They say they don't do drama, but everyone around knows they love it.

Administrator "A" has no time for nonsense. They handle situations quickly and move on. Administrator "B" beats even the slightest situation into the ground.

Dr. Andrews was definitely a "B." She loved drama. It was probably the drama that brought her demise in the district. Even though she was moving on to "bigger and better" opportunities.

On the day class placements were communicated to teachers, Dr. Andrews called in Phyllis Langdon. Phyllis had been teaching third grade for numerous years and had been a district worker for over ten years. When Phyllis walked into the office, she knew something was up. What grade would she be teaching the following year? Phyllis could see Mrs. Baker moving things around her desk and not making any eye contact. This couldn't be good. Wide-eyed Mrs. Baker was understandable. This was terrifying.

Phyllis went into Dr. Andrews's office and was asked to close the door. There was no idle chitchat. Dr. Andrews went into full administrator role.

Phyllis tried not to worry too much. She had just signed her year-end evaluation the day before, and it had been a glowing review. So Phyllis was prepared for a grade change and would deal with it. But what she wasn't prepared for was what Dr. Andrews had to say.

As if she were reading things off a grocery list, Dr. Andrews told Phyllis that she would no longer be teaching third grade. Phyllis would now be teaching kindergarten, but in another building. News like this comes as a major blow to staff members. Changing a grade is one thing, but a different location? That's a huge deal.

There really wasn't much reason for the move. Dr. Andrews was always repeating meaningless taglines like, "The change will be good." Or "Sometimes people make a better fit elsewhere."

Phyllis quickly removed herself and went back to her classroom. There was no doubt that Mrs. Baker knew all about it by the expression on her face as Phyllis was leaving the office. "Call the next person down," is what Phyllis heard Dr. Andrews utter to Mrs. Baker as she walked out of the office.

Situations like this were very common with Dr. Andrews. She had done the same thing two years before to another seasoned teacher. Poor Desiree Walters had worked over twenty-five years at that school and was suddenly told she had to relocate to another building.

Dr. Andrews began by praising the wonderful job Desiree was doing and the great year she'd had. Then Dr. Andrews dropped the bomb that Desiree would be moving on to another building. The biggest slap in the face was that there were a handful of new teachers who were taking over classroom positions.

Really? There's no room for Desiree in the building when there are numerous openings? Do administrators think they're fooling anyone? What they're doing is making themselves look like fools.

This is the nonsense that has plagued school districts for decades, and it's just getting worse. If administrators want to get their own people in, they simply move the people they think they can get away with moving without concern for that teacher's experience, relationships, or convenience.

Does the administration think they're fooling anyone with the bullshit that flies from their mouths? Do they realize how ridiculous they look? Where's their integrity? Why don't they actually stand up for their staff? Unfortunately, this was what five years with Dr. Andrews had been like.

The biggest farce was how she talked about it after lowering the boom on teachers like Phyllis and Desiree. She would tell staff the reason for these moves was because "We do 'What's Best for Children' here!" A wonderful phrase with such a beautiful meaning had become twisted into a sick joke every time it was echoed throughout the building. It needed to stop. Either use the phrase appropriately or don't use it at all.

Sharon would bellow at grade level meetings to teachers across the district. "What's best for children? What's best for children? If they really believed that, then why did *this* happen, or why was *that* allowed to go on for so long? What's best for children? What a joke."

Once again, colleagues would be in full agreement and instead of meeting to discuss their training or whatever the meeting had been called for, it became a gripe session. A chance to hash over all the blunders that were most definitely *not* best for children.

In the end, these gripe sessions were a boon to the teachers. It reminded everyone that they were in it together. They all felt the same way. They were all in the same boat. A sinking one, but at least they weren't alone in it. "Life preservers for everyone," is what Carol Moss, a teacher from another building, would say.

Alice and Anna were two rare teachers who didn't get involved in the gripe sessions at their grade level meetings. It's not that they weren't in agreement, they just didn't feel the need to work themselves up over it. Sadly, teachers like Alice and Anna were becoming a thing of the past. Teachers who just focused on their students and nothing else. They let the nonsense they could do nothing about roll off their shoulders.

The one good thing about Dr. Andrews was that she occasionally did something right. Maybe during her five-year reign, she did one or two things that made the rest of the staff quite happy with her.

Dr. Andrews kept everything you said to her in her head. Usually no action would be taken, but at least you got it off your chest. The one thing to keep in mind, however, was that if you had a complaint about a fellow colleague, you didn't want to be the only one to bring it before her. It was always best to meet with Dr. Andrews in a group if there was a complaint about something or someone in the building.

Teachers in every district around the country can always point to at least one person in the building whose job responsibilities are questioned daily. You know the type. You ask them to assist you with something that is in their area of expertise, but they'll help you when they're good and ready. You'll ask for something important for you and your class, but it will take a month for it to be done. Something that could have been done in fifteen minutes.

Things of this nature are always whispered into administrators' ears. They know when staff members are being difficult with colleagues and not doing their job the way they're supposed to. The biggest problem is that some administrators are no help in these situations. Instead of taking care of it immediately, they try to be nice and ask politely for the job to be done in an email. Whatever happened to going to the source of the problem and saying, "This needs to be done, now!"

No matter who wasn't doing what they were supposed to be doing, and especially if it was hindering other teachers from moving forward in their classrooms, Dr. Andrews wanted to know about it.

While you almost never want to see a fellow staff member moved out of the building, once in a very great while there is a case that brings a smile to your face. And for once, Dr. Andrews got it right. It might have taken her a whole year of listening to staff complain about a colleague's attitude, but she took care of it at the beginning of a new school year, telling this person that they would now be assisting staff in another building.

Sadly, these situations can almost always be avoided if handled immediately after one or two complaints. The constant walking on eggshells has to stop, especially in a work environment where there are children. These people need to be spoken to and made aware of how they're conducting themselves and how they need to be a productive part of the team. Directly and specifically point out the challenges they're causing and then give them suggestions and opportunities for improvement. In some cases, there will be no change. Some people are just plain miserable in their jobs. Yes, it could stem from their home life, but that shouldn't come with them to work.

Administrators can have a tough time dealing with staff. It's a balancing act. But when staff have justifiable complaints or a request that needs to be handled, action ought to be taken immediately. The bullies are not just on the playground. It shouldn't take a year, or years in some cases, to deal with it.

Anna and Alice always wondered if those bullies ever put two and two together and wondered if their actions in the past had something to do with their current situation. It's probably good food for thought for all staff members. What goes around does come around eventually. And when it finally does, the relief among the rest of the staff is palpable.

All aspects in a school setting directly relate back to doing what's best for children. Materials, school safety, social and emotional training, and even class placements.

Sharon was always on top of this each school year. For years, Sharon would get "socked," as they would say, with a class that could make even the most experienced teacher want to call it quits. If there was a discipline problem or a parent issue in the grade, you could find it in Sharon's room.

This was yet another example of administration delegating responsibilities to staff who should never be expected to deal with that kind of thing.

Each year Sharon's new class never looked the way Courtney and her grade level partners had recommended. It's the classroom teacher who knows their students better than anyone else. They spend over thirty-five hours a week with them. They know what students can remain together and which ones should be separated for the sanity of the next year's teacher.

But when administrators let everyone stick their noses into it, they invariably create multiple situations that are not the best for the children. Putting a child into a class with another child who antagonizes them all year long is unacceptable. Classroom teachers know best when it comes to their students; it just seems some staff members have a hard time figuring that out.

Sharon continually reminds her colleagues of the year a girl had been put into her class without a single one of the girl's friends from her previous class. All of this young child's friends from the third grade were scattered among the other fourth grade classes, and she didn't have a friend with her at all. So who do you think hears about this severe blunder from the outraged parent when the new school year begins? Sharon has to deal with it. It's not the way you want to start off a school year with new-to-you parents. It's not good for anyone, including the administrator.

Sharon had no doubt that Courtney and her grade level partners had recommended a very different class group. It was the interference of other staff members that caused these situations. Cronyism is a big problem when the wrong people are put in charge of class placements. Someone wants to make sure that certain teachers get the best of the classes. Could it be because they're friends outside of work? You'd better believe it. Could it be because a teacher told someone they didn't want to be in the same classroom with a certain student because they're not very fond of them from the year before? You'd better believe it.

More administrators need to take the tagline much more seriously. Remember, it's not "What's Best for Teachers." It's "What's Best for *Children*."

TIMES, THEY ARE A-CHANGIN'

Alice and Anna were starting to feel it. They would talk about retiring and had agreed they would do it together. Retiring was a difficult decision for many of their previous colleagues. They both knew they would be fine with it when the time arrived. They knew they would have many things to keep them busy. You can't retire and do nothing because that only leads to sadness and depression. It's a decision that needs to be thought out very carefully.

Both Alice and Anna knew things were never going to go back to the good old days. Sure, they could do things their way in their classrooms, but the outside world was in constant change. Kids will always be kids. How they were being raised had changed for many, but not all of them. There were still many wonderful families bringing up their children with the same morals and respect as families of the past.

Alice and Anna wanted to enjoy their retirement. They saw way too many colleagues who waited too long to retire and, sadly, passed away only a few years into that special time. The two would decide soon enough, but until then, they focused on other things.

Mia's baby shower was a success. The staff showered her with generous gifts for her coming baby. Occasions of this nature tended to ease the tensions of the daily nonsense that fills the hallways of schools around the country. Celebrations of new babies and upcoming weddings washed away the ongoing routines of teaching.

As Mia opened her gifts, you could feel the rumblings of the countdown to the last day of school. By June, both teachers and students were ready to take a break from the daily grind and, in some cases, from each other. End-of-year paperwork, report cards, and classroom clean-up were all part of this time of year. If you got lucky, the days of June wouldn't get too humid yet, which would make the final weeks bearable. But nine out of ten times, luck ran out when it came to that.

Sharon never understood why she had to pack up her whole classroom. The only thing that would be done in her classroom over the summer was her floors. She would just have to pull everything out and set it up all over again in approximately eight weeks anyway. She always hoped that someone with some brains would step up to the plate and see how ridiculous this was, but she knew there was no real hope of that.

As the final week of the school year arrived, everyone's face was showing wear and tear. Keeping the students focused was nearly impossible. Creative activities, games, and a year-end party are what help everyone get through it.

The last day of school is filled with mixed emotions. It all depended on the group you had just spent the last ten months with. There were some years when Alice and Anna would practically race to get to the dismissal doors first. And then there were the years when you didn't want to let go of one of the nicest groups of children you'd ever worked with. It certainly didn't make it easier for what was heading your way in September.

All the teachers, with their students in tow, made their way to the dismissal doors. Parents would be waiting to begin their new daily routine for the next ten weeks. In the good old days, students would open their report cards and see who their teacher would be the following year. But like so many traditions, this one had been killed, along with so many other things in the world of education. Yet another potential problem that was pushed aside for as long as possible. Something else to deal with at the end of August, when there's a million and one other things to do.

As families dispersed from the school, most of the colleagues made a mad dash for their cars. It's a feeling only a teacher can fully understand.

Courtney said her round of goodbyes and headed back to her classroom. While some of her colleagues would leave with just a pocketbook in hand, Courtney would be lugging home stacks of books so she could start planning for the fall. Yes, teachers work over the summer, as well. Courtney had an uncle who always told her she "had it made" with all these vacations. She knew it was something many people believed. But these dolts had no idea what the responsibilities of a dedicated teacher were all about. Courtney knew not all teachers were like her, but she wasn't pointing fingers. She would leave that to Sharon.

22 YEARS LATER . . . REFLECTIONS

Where had the last twenty-two years gone? With an iced coffee in hand, Courtney took a solo tour of the place where she'd taught for the last thirty years. It was one final walk up and down the stairs and across all the floors of the building. She regretted not keeping track of her steps for all those years. In any event, it was time for Courtney Michaels to retire. That's right, she was no longer Courtney Reynolds.

It happened twelve years ago. She finally met her Mr. Right.

Scott Michaels was a banker. They met at the wedding of a mutual friend, and the rest, as they say, is history. Scott was a sweet man who stood at a mere five foot, six inches. So much for her frequent dreams of men of an extreme height.

Scott was going to be retiring too. They were looking forward to spending time doing the things they enjoyed doing together. It felt like the perfect time.

As she sat in her classroom, she thought back to many of the colleagues who had come and gone.

She was still friends with Alice and Anna, who were now in their seventies. A get-together dinner would happen every once in a while, a chance to catch up and reminisce about the past, usually resulting in roars of laughter.

Mia was now married with three children. She never went back to teaching after she had her first child. She wanted to stay home and, financially, she could. Courtney had watched Mia's children grow up via yearly Christmas cards.

Sharon was now a widow. Her husband, Ed, had passed suddenly, two years after she retired. Everyone still heard from her, and she spent most of her days babysitting her grandchildren and probably helping them with their homework, her way.

As Courtney dismissed her last class for the last time, the emotions hit hard. A quick sprint to her classroom to compose herself was in order.

The good news is she would stay in touch with the people who really mattered. She would stay in touch with the colleagues she was close to. When Courtney told them she would keep connected and get together, she would.

She was always amazed when she would ask other retirees if they'd heard from those "friends" they were supposedly so close to in school. The usual response was, "I never hear from them." When Courtney Reynolds Michaels said something, she meant it.

It was now time for the last ride home on the road Courtney had traveled back and forth on for thirty years. She would take it slow and give herself some time to reflect on what she had accomplished. To think about the people she'd known and dealt with for all those years. Also, she thought about what advice she would give to brand new teachers and to those she had left behind.

Courtney believed you close your door and do your job. Block out the nonsense that occurs outside of your own classroom. Your classroom is another home for your students. Make it a happy, calming, fun-filled learning environment that any child would want to be in. Spending time talking about other colleagues or being negative just oozes back into a peaceful classroom. Avoid spending time with the teachers who do that—you know who they are.

Courtney would tell her colleagues not to be *that* educator who has to have an opinion on everything. Don't be the person who makes meetings go long because you have more to say. We all know who those people are. Don't be that person. Are you aware that half the people in the room are texting each other with comments saying, "Is she for real?" "Doesn't she know we all want to leave?" "Can you spell o-b-l-i-v-i-o-u-s?"

Courtney would also tell people there's life outside of school. You need to have other hobbies aside from your passion for teaching. A teacher with interests in a variety of areas brings that knowledge to their classroom. There's so much more for children to learn beyond what's in a curriculum guide.

Also, to those colleagues who always seem angry at the world, what's the point? Sure, everyone has bad days, and we don't know what goes on in one's home, but don't be that person who spews anger at others for no reason or constantly talks about people behind their backs. Usually, those people are unhappy about themselves and are jealous of someone else. Always know that it's a waste of precious time. You jump ahead to many years later, and those people are no longer on this earth. Was all that meanness and anger really worth it? It's been said that anger eats away at you. Maybe it does.

Finally, be a professional and act like one. As the years rolled by, you could always count on Sharon to show disgust at how some teachers would show up to work. "Did she just roll out of bed?" "Does that teacher even own a comb?" And her biggest pet peeve: "Doesn't she know what time she's supposed to be here?" That was a question that could be asked of a surprising number of teachers. Why are there always a few colleagues, some not even tenured, allowed to arrive late almost every day? The teacher who has a husband and four children knows how to get to school in plenty of time and is never late. This is one way in which the administrators show they don't truly care about the morale of the other staff members. They see it going on, yet they do nothing.

But this was the beginning of a new chapter in the life of Courtney Reynolds Michaels. She'll remember the good times. She'll remember the names of her students who were a gift from God—and try to forget those who seemed to be a gift from the devil. She'll cherish the friendships she made that will continue on for the rest of her life. But most importantly, she will confidently believe that she always did what was best for the children.

ABOUT THE AUTHOR

John Contratti was an elementary school teacher for thirty-two years. He's the author of two children's books, *Cooking with Mr. C.* and *Mr. C. Takes Manhattan*, and the cookbook, *J. C. In The Kitchen*. He has appeared on the television dramas *The Americans*, *Royal Pains*, and the Hallmark Channel cooking program, *Mad Hungry with Lucinda Scala Quinn*, which was produced by Martha Stewart. He is currently the host of the successful podcast, *Up Next with John Contratti*. He is a supporter of the organizations Keen Company and Broadway Cares. Contratti resides in New York, New York.